My Postman Pat Storytime Book

Stories by John Cunliffe
Pictures by Celia Berridge
from the original television designs by Ivor Wood

TREASURE PRESS

POSTMAN PAT'S FOGGY DAY and POSTMAN PAT'S DIFFICULT DAY
First published 1982 by André Deutsch Limited
Text Copyright © 1982 by John Cunliffe
Illustrations Copyright © 1982 by Celia Berridge and Ivor Wood

POSTMAN PAT TAKES A MESSAGE and POSTMAN PAT'S TRACTOR EXPRESS
First published 1983 by André Deutsch Limited
Text Copyright © 1983 by John Cunliffe
Illustrations Copyright © 1983 by Celia Berridge and Ivor Wood

POSTMAN PAT'S LETTERS ON ICE and POSTMAN PAT'S BREEZY DAY
First published 1985 by André Deutsch Limited
Text Copyright © 1985 by John Cunliffe
Illustrations Copyright © 1985 by Celia Berridge and Woodland Animations Limited

First published in this format in 1986
under the title *Another Big Postman Pat Storybook*

This edition published in 1987 by
Treasure Press
Michelin House
81 Fulham Road
London SW3 6RB
by arrangement with André Deutsch Limited

Reprinted 1988, 1989

Text Copyright © by John Cunliffe 1982, 1983 and 1985
Illustrations Copyright © Celia Berridge and Ivor
Wood 1982 and 1983, Celia Berridge and Woodland Animations 1985
All rights reserved

ISBN 1850512345

Printed in Czechoslovakia by TSNP Martin
50667/3

CONTENTS

Postman Pat's
Foggy Day

There was thick fog in Greendale. Postman Pat had to go slowly along the winding lanes.

"This is nasty," said Pat.

Jess fluffed up his fur; he didn't like the fog either – it made a cold and clinging wetness in the air.

Pat was late when he reached the village post-office. Mrs. Goggins was busy dusting the shelves.

"Good morning, Mrs. Goggins!" called Pat. "Sorry I'm late – it's this blessed fog."

"No need to hurry," said Mrs. Goggins. "There's no sign of the letters yet. The fog's made you late; it will make the letters late, too. Come in and sit down, and have a cup of tea."

Pat went into Mrs. Goggins' sitting-room, at the back of the shop. There were big armchairs and a blazing fire. Pat warmed his hands and sat back amongst the cushions. Jess curled up near the fire and purred.

"I'll just brew up," said Mrs. Goggins.

"Thank you," said Pat; "this is lovely."

Pat was just getting warm and comfortable, and Mrs. Goggins was just bringing the tea and biscuits, when PING went the shop's door-bell.

"It's early for a customer," said Mrs. Goggins.

"That's a good cup of tea," said Pat. But Mrs. Goggins came in with the mailbag, saying, "It's here!"

Pat was surprised. "What already? Just as I've picked my favourite biscuit, too. No time for that, now. I'd better be on my way. Come on, Jess."

He went into the shop and helped Mrs. Goggins to sort the letters. Then out into the fog again, and Pat was on his way. He knew the Greendale roads well enough, but they looked different in the fog.

He went the wrong way somewhere, so he stopped to look at a signpost. But it wasn't a signpost; only a crossroads sign. Now what? Pat didn't know which way to go. He walked along the lane, trying to see where he was.

Then he saw someone standing in the field. He said, "Why is he so still? It must be Ted Glen, out after rabbits. He'll know the way. I'll pop over with his letter and ask him."

Pat walked across the field very quietly, so as not to frighten the rabbits away.
He touched Ted on the shoulder.
Ted didn't move.
He put the letter in Ted's pocket.
Still Ted did not move.

He gave Ted a nudge.

Ted swung round suddenly! Oh! It wasn't Ted at all! It was a scarecrow. Pat did feel silly. He said, "Sorry, scarecrow, the letter isn't for you, and I don't suppose you can tell me the way in this fog. Goodbye!"

Pat walked back to the road. He was wondering what to do, when he saw lights coming through the fog. It was Alf Thompson on his tractor. Luckily, *he* wasn't lost; he soon showed Pat which way to go.

Pat was on his way again. His next stop was at the church. The Reverend Timms met him at the door. He said, "Hello, Pat. Isn't this fog ghastly! I don't know how you find the way. It's choir-practice, too. I expect Miss Hubbard will come; nothing stops her. Three letters, to-day? Thanks, Pat. Now go carefully, and trust in the Lord. Goodbye!"

"Cheerio, Reverend."

When Pat looked in his van, Jess had gone! He looked everywhere – under the van, behind the van, over the wall. There was no sign of Jess. Where could that cat be? He called – "Jess! Jess!" There was no answer. Perhaps Jess had gone looking for rabbits? Pat set out to seek him.

He called and called and called –

"Jess! Jess! Where are you?" He went over a stile, and across a field; through a gate, through a small wood, into another field, calling all the time, "Where are you, Jess? Jess! Jess! Come on, Jess. Here, puss: silly puss – this is no time for hide-and-seek."

He sat down on a tussock to rest. He put his hand on something furry. It moved!

"Oh!" What a fright it gave him. It was Jess!

"Jess, you silly cat. Where have you been?"

Jess was cold and wet; Pat could not be too cross with him. He gave him a cuddle, then tucked him under his arm, saying, "Come on, Jess. We'd better be on our way. Now, let's see, which way is it . . . .?"

Pat was lost again and the fog was thicker than ever.

"Now you've done it, Jess. We're really lost this time."

Pat began to wander about in the fog. He couldn't find the road, let alone his van.

He walked into mud, up to his ankles.

13

Then he stumbled through a stream and a patch of nettles. The branches of a tree scratched his face and knocked his hat off. The fog swirled round him. He was lost, and more surely lost with every step.

Not so very far away, Miss Hubbard was cycling along the road. When she saw Pat's van, she stopped and looked inside.

"No Pat? No Jess?" she said. "I wonder if they are in the church?"

There was only the Reverend Timms in the church, sorting out the hymn books.

"Hello, vicar," said Miss Hubbard. "Have you seen Pat? His van's outside, and there's no sign of him or his cat. Whatever can have happened to them?"

"Dear me," said the Reverend Timms. "Pat called some time ago. They must be lost in the fog."

"I know what we must do," said Miss Hubbard. "We must ring the bells to guide them back to the church."

And that is what they did. They pulled the ropes, and the bells clanged and clamoured in the church-tower.

15

Out in the misty fields, Pat stopped to listen.

"Bells?" he said. "I thought it was a *choir*-practice. I wonder what they're ringing for? They're as good as a fog-horn. We'll soon find the way, now."

Pat followed the sound. The way went through a bramble-patch and some *very* prickly gorse; but it wasn't long before he found the road, then his van, then the church.

The church door opened, and in came Pat, blinking in the light.

"There's Pat!" cried Miss Hubbard, and they stopped ringing.

"Hello," said Pat. "It's a good thing you rang those bells. We were properly lost.
Never mind – we're all right now."

"The good Lord will be our guide," said the Reverend Timms. "Come and have some tea; there's plenty in the pot."

"Thanks – I need it," said Pat. There was milk for Jess.

They talked of other foggy days they had known, and enjoyed their tea.

Then, Miss Hubbard said, "Look at the windows!" The coloured glass was shining quite brightly. "It's much brighter outside." They went to the door.

A breeze was blowing the fog away and the sun was beginning to shine. They could see the fields and hills again.

"That's *much* better," said Pat. "Now I can get on with my letters. Come on, Jess.
Cheerio! Thanks for the tea!"

Pat waved goodbye and went on his way. It was lovely driving along in the sunshine, without getting lost. They passed the scarecrow, standing patiently in its field.

"Look, Jess," said Pat. "That scarecrow's still waiting for a letter."
Jess was hoping there would be rabbit-pie for tea.

Postman Pat's
Difficult Day

It was a lovely morning in Greendale. The sun was shining. The birds were singing. Where was Postman Pat? It was long past his time to be up and on his way, but his curtains were closed and his van stood outside. All was silent and still. Then . . . the door opened and Pat looked out. He looked sleepily at his watch. "Oh dear, is it *that* time?"

He dressed and rushed out without any breakfast, and without his hat! He dashed back for his hat, fell over his cat, and landed in a heap on the doorstep.

He picked Jess up and ran to his van, saying, "Come on, let's get moving, Jess. We're ever so late."

He talked to Jess as they drove along the winding roads.
"What a start to the day! I wonder why that blooming alarm-clock didn't go off? We'll have to see if Ted can mend it."

Mrs. Goggins was having a difficult morning, too. She was trying to mend a parcel. It was for Ted Glen. When Pat arrived he tried to help, but they got all tangled up in sticky tape! What a muddle!

"I do wish people would wrap parcels up properly," said Mrs. Goggins. "This is in a right old mess – and heavy, too. I don't know what Ted will say."

"It's just one of those days," said Pat. "First I slept in, because my alarm didn't go off, then this parcel. Never mind, it's a lovely morning. Cheerio!"

Pat was on his way. He saw Ted, mending a fence on the hillside.

"Hello," he said, "there's Ted. I'll give him his parcel before it falls to bits."

He stopped and shouted to Ted, "Hi! Ted – there's a parcel for you."

Ted came down the hill. Pat passed the parcel to him over the wall. He was just saying, "Be careful, Ted, it's a bit loose," when . . . "Oooooooooops!" it slipped, and Ted dropped it.

"Oh *no!*"

Dozens of little balls, and wheels, and screws, rolled away into the grass. Ted, on his hands and knees, began to scratch and search for them.

"Nay," he said, "I'll never find them in all this long grass."

"Hold on," said Pat, climbing over the wall, "I'll give you a hand."

"It's hopeless," said Ted.

When Bill Thompson saw them, he came over to see what they were doing.

"I have just the thing," he said. It was a large magnet. It picked up all the wheels, and balls, and screws from the grass.

"I hope they're all there," said Pat.
"I'll count them," said Ted. "Thanks."
"Cheerio Ted."
"Cheerio Pat."
Ted said, "Thanks," to Bill; "That was real handy."

Pat's next stop was at Thompson Ground. Alf was up a ladder, mending the barn wall. Pat was walking under the ladder, when Alf shouted, "Look out!"
   Too late!

"Ooooooooohhhhh! Ouch!" said Pat.
   Alf had dropped his tin of nails. Pat tried to catch it – twisted round – lost his balance – and sat down with a bump, with his hand twisted under him. Alf came down the ladder.
   "You all right, Pat?"
   "No, I think I've sprained my wrist."
   "I'll go and get a bandage," said Alf.

Then Mrs. Thompson came along.

"Dear me, whatever have you been up to, Pat?"

"Just in too much of a hurry," said Pat. "Walking under ladders."

Mrs. Thompson looked at his wrist. "Now hold still," she said, "and I'll bind it up for you. But you won't be able to drive any more to-day, you know. You'll have to rest it."

"What about all my letters?" said Pat.

Sam Waldron arrived in his mobile-shop. They told him about Pat's accident.

"Why don't you put your letters and parcels in my van?" said Sam. "We can do our rounds together."

"And the post will get through after all," said Pat. "Thanks, Sam; it's a grand idea."

Everyone helped to move the parcels and letters into Sam's van.

"There's plenty of room," said Sam. "Just stack them at the back of the van behind the seats."

"Come on, Jess," said Mrs. Thompson. She put Jess on the seat. "You'll be all right in there."

Pat climbed in beside Sam, and Jess curled up on his knee.

"Off we go," said Sam.

Away they went.

"What a surprise everyone will get, when they see us together," said Pat. And so they did.

Pat's hand was still hurting, so they made their first stop at Dr. Gilbertson's house.

She had a good look at his hand, and said, "It's not broken. You'll be all right in a day or two. I'll just give you something to soothe it."

She gave him a jar of cream that took the pain away.

"Thank you, doctor," said Pat. "Cheerio!"

On they went to Greendale Farm.

"What a good idea," said Mrs. Pottage, when she saw them. "We can get our post and parcels with our potatoes and peas."

All the people of Greendale agreed with her, as Pat and Sam went on their way. The Reverend Timms . . . Miss Hubbard . . . Granny Dryden . . . George Lancaster . . . Peter Fogg . . . and all the children.

Jess liked Sam's van, too, because the smell of fish tickled his nose. At the end of the day, Sam gave Jess a kipper all to himself, and that turned a difficult day into a perfect day, as far as Jess was concerned.

Postman Pat
Takes a Message

The wind had been blowing and banging all night in Greendale. When morning came, Postman Pat set out on his round. He drove his red van and his cat, Jess, sat by his side. What a mess the wind had made!

All along the valley, branches had been blown off the trees. Many were scattered on the roads and Pat had to dodge the big ones as he drove along. By Greendale Farm, a whole tree had blown down, just missing Peter Fogg's cottage. Some telephone-wires were broken too.

"Dear me," said Pat, "that's a nuisance. There'll be a fair number of telephones out of action, now."

Then, as they came to the vicarage, he stopped.
"I wonder if the Reverend kept that stamp for me? Better pop in and see him . . . I hope he remembered."
The Reverend Timms was busy. He seemed to be packing his cases to go on holiday.

"Hello, Reverend!" called Pat. "I just popped in to see if you kept that Australian stamp for me, yesterday."

"Of course, Pat," said the Reverend Timms, "just the thing for your collection . . ."

"Thanks," said Pat, "but where are you off to?"

"I'm off to London! To meet my sister, Elsie . . . that's what the letter was all about . . . she's flying over from Australia . . . haven't seen her for years . . . what a rush! Now, *where* did I put that stamp? Ah, *here* it is."

"Thank you," said Pat.

The Reverend picked the telephone up to see if it was working. No luck! "Such a nuisance," he said. "The phone's not working, so I'll have to rush round and see everyone, to cancel the church meetings while I'm away. Such a bother, with a train to catch . . ."

"It's this wind," said Pat. "It's brought the wires down."

"Well, I'll just have to hurry. The train goes at ten o'clock."

"I hope you get round in time," said Pat. "Cheerio! Have a good trip! Thanks for the stamp!"

Pat was on his way.

He called at the post-office for the letters.

"Morning, Mrs. Goggins! I'm not late, am I?"

"Not really," said Mrs. Goggins, "but I thought you might have trouble getting through, what with all these trees being blown down."

Pat told Mrs. Goggins about the Reverend Timms' letter, and his trip to London, and his telephone being out of order.

"Ee it's a bad job, isn't it," she said. Then her telephone began to ring.

"*My* phone's working, anyway. Hello – Greendale post-office here – who is it? Elsie Timms? Urgent message for the Reverend Timms? Yes . . . his phone *is* out of order . . . yes . . . your flight diverted to Manchester?"

"Oh dear," said Pat.

"You'll come on to Greendale by car? Yes . . . I'll ask our postman to dash over and tell the Reverend not to go to London after all – he might just catch him."

40

"I've got the message," said Pat. "Tell her I'm on my way."
"Bye, Pat! I hope you're on time. Bye!"
Pat dashed out to his van.
"Hold tight, Jess; it's full speed ahead."

Along the twisting roads they went, back to the vicarage. Pat knocked on the door, but the vicar had gone.

"I'll leave a note for him," said Pat, "in case he calls back before he catches his train. Let's see, he's sure to call on Miss Hubbard. We'll try and catch up with him there. Come on, Jess, we can take a short cut along the back road."

41

Pat jolted off along the bumpy back road to Miss Hubbard's. It was a very rough ride. And then, when they were almost there, the road was blocked by Peter Fogg's trailer. There wasn't even enough room to turn round and go back. So Pat jumped out, put Jess in his bag, and ran across the field to Miss Hubbard's cottage.

"Hello, Pat," said Miss Hubbard, "what's all the hurry, and where is your van?"

"Morning, Miss Hubbard," Pat panted, "I'm trying to catch up with the Reverend Timms. Have you seen him?"

"Oh, he went a few minutes ago. He's in a hurry too; he wants to catch a train."

"I must catch him before he does," said Pat. "I have an urgent message for him."

"He did say he was calling on Ted Glen. You might catch him there. Quick! You can borrow my bike. Go on!"

Pat put Jess in the basket, and wobbled away, gathering speed. He called over his shoulder –

"Thanks, Miss Hubbard! I'll try anything . . . hold tight, Jess!"

Pat whizzed, and jolted, and wobbled his way to Ted Glen's; but he couldn't stop when he arrived, and he crashed into the workshop-door, and tumbled in a heap on the floor.

"Hello, Pat, whatever are you doing?" said Ted. "Are you all right?"

"Yes, I think so. I'm trying to catch up with the Reverend."

"You're too late," said Ted. "The Reverend's gone; but he said he would call on Granny Dryden, before he catches his train." But when Pat tried the bike, the front wheel wouldn't go round.

"Leave it to me," said Ted. "I'll fettle it. You can borrow these roller-skates. I've just mended them. You'll fairly move when you get these on."

"Well, I said I'd try anything," said Pat, "and we must catch the Reverend before he catches his train. Thanks, Ted. Here we go again . . . Ooooooooooops!"

Pat shot out of Ted's workshop like a rocket, and away along the road to Granny Dryden's. *But*, he had forgotten to ask Ted where the brakes were! When he came to a sharp bend in the road, he was going too fast to get round the bend, and too fast to stop. So he did a somersault over the gate and landed in a soft patch of mud.

Sam Waldron's van was coming along the road. The Reverend Timms was riding in it, as Sam was giving him a lift to the station.

"I thought I saw Pat dive over that gate," said Sam. He stopped his van to get a better look.

Then, Pat scrambled to his feet and waved to them.

"It *is* Pat," said Sam.

"Hello, Sam! . . . and Reverend!" called Pat. "I've caught you at last. Thank goodness you've not gone to London."

Pat told the Reverend all about his sister's phone message, and how he must not go to London after all, as she was coming straight to Greendale.

"Lord bless us," he said, "what a good thing you caught me in time. I'd have gone traipsing off to London and missed Elsie, and she would have been here looking for me! After all that rush, too! Never mind, all's well in the end. Thank you so much, Pat. Let's go home, Sam, and we'll have a nice cup of tea. Can we give you a lift, Pat?"

But Peter Fogg came along, with his tractor and trailer. When he heard the story, he said,

"It's my fault that Pat had to leave his van. I left my trailer in the road. I'll give you a lift back to your van, Pat."

"And I'd better get along to meet my sister," said the Reverend Timms. "God speed! And thanks to all!"

So Pat and Jess rode back on the trailer. Pat was glad to see his van again. As for Jess, he never wanted to see a bike or a roller-skate again. He curled up thankfully on his seat, as Pat drove on his way. As they passed the vicarage, the Reverend was just carrying a suitcase in, with an Australian label on it.

"She's arrived," he said. "I was back just in time, thanks to you, Pat. And I found your pen on my doorstep."

"Thanks," said Pat. "I hope your sister enjoys her visit. Cheerio!"

"Thanks, Pat. Bye! Bye, Jess!"

"Now we'll get the letters delivered," said Pat to Jess. "That bothersome wind – it's made a real mischief of itself, to-day."

Postman Pat's
Tractor Express

Every summer, visitors came to Greendale, to walk in the hills and camp in the meadows.

   "What lovely weather for people on holiday," said Pat, as he drove along the valley.

He called at the village post-office, to collect the day's post.

"Morning, Mrs. Goggins! Fine day!"

"Morning, Pat! Yes, and a busy one, too," said Mrs. Goggins. "Plenty of post for the visitors. The Jacksons are staying up at Birk Howe Cottage. There are some letters for them, so don't forget the extra call, will you, Pat? Oh yes, and there's a *registered* letter for those campers up at Southlands Farm. They'll have to sign for that, of course. I do hope you catch them in. *And* a parcel for Granny Dryden; I wonder what that can be?"

"It's a busy time, with all these people on holiday," said Pat. "I'll be glad when it's my holiday."

"Have a good day, Pat," said Mrs. Goggins.

"Cheerio!"

Pat was on his way.

He delivered his letters all along the valley.

All was quiet at Birk Howe Cottage. The Jacksons were away, and the only sound was the humming of flies and bees in the beautiful garden. But someone had left a gate open. And something unfortunate happened . . .

Some sheep were nibbling the dry grasses outside the garden. Then, one of them found the open gate and wandered in. The grass in the garden was freshly watered and green. Lovely! The sheep began to crop the grass, trampling flowers down as it went. Two more sheep pushed through the gate, then another; then more and more, until they were all in, almost twenty of them!

They trampled, and nibbled, and pushed, and bleated joyously. They smashed down the flowers, ate all the lettuces, and broke a trellis. One put its foot through the glass in a cold-frame. What a mess they made in that lovely garden!

They were like a bunch of woolly hooligans. Then Peter Fogg came along, and shouted at them over the wall, but it was too late. He ran into the garden and began to chase them out. What a time he had! They hid behind hedges and dodged round trellises – they didn't want to go.

Then Pat arrived with the letters and came to help. He had chased sheep before. It took them a long time to get all the sheep out, and the garden was ruined.

"What a mess," said Peter. "It'll take the Jacksons the rest of their holiday to get this garden tidied up!"

"It isn't your fault," said Pat. "People should close gates properly in the country. I bet they'll not do that again."

"No, I don't think they will," said Peter. "Anyway, thanks for helping. Cheerio!"

Pat's next stop was at Granny Dryden's cottage.

She was so pleased to see her parcel, that she opened it there and then. It was her new catalogue from Manchester. It was full of pictures of things to buy.

"Is there anything you'd like to order?" she asked Pat.

"Let's have a look," said Pat, turning the pages.

He chose a digital watch, with a musical alarm.

"*That's* a funny watch," said Granny Dryden. "It doesn't look like a watch at all to me."

"Oh, it's a good one," said Pat. "It doesn't even need winding. It will help to keep me on time. Goodbye!"

Pat was on his way.

He had to go up the hill to Intake Farm with a letter for George Lancaster. George didn't often get letters, so he was very pleased to see this one.

"You'll be passing the campers, won't you?" said George. "Could you take them some eggs?"

"Yes, that's all right," said Pat. "I have a letter for them, so I'll have to stop there, anyway."

George went for the eggs.

"What beauties" said Pat. "I must take care not to drop them, specially as they're all in one basket . . . Cheerio!"

Pat was off again. He soon spotted the tents in the field, and stopped his van by the gate. But the tent's flaps were all zipped up and all was quiet.

Pat called,

"Hello! Anyone at home?"

But there was no answer.

"That's a nuisance – they must have gone off for a walk. Well, I can tuck the eggs under here. They'll be all right."

He put the basket of eggs in the shade, under the tent's fly-sheet.

"But what about this registered letter? I can't leave that, it looks too valuable, and they'll have to sign for it. I wonder if Miss Hubbard knows where they've gone?"

Miss Hubbard's cottage was just across the field. So Pat walked over, to see if she was at home. He was lucky – she had just cycled back from the village. Pat told her about the special letter; she knew where the campers were, all right.

"They've gone off to see the Gategill Waterfalls. They asked me the way this morning."

"Oh dear," said Pat, "that's at least six miles, and my van can't go along that old track."

"I'll borrow a tractor from the farm," said Miss Hubbard.

"Er . . . I can't drive a tractor," said Pat.

"Don't worry, I can," Miss Hubbard said; and off she went, for the tractor.

Pat wasn't sure that he wanted to ride on a tractor; but there was no other way. So he climbed on, and off they went. It was a very exciting ride . . . and a rough one in places. The track was all bends, and bumps, and holes.

There were loose places, where they went sliding and skidding. There were boggy places, where they squelched and splashed mud. They had to duck under low branches of trees, and Pat had to keep jumping down to open and close gates. He was glad when they arrived, but he was almost too sore and stiff to get off and take the letter to the campers.

But he struggled over the rocks to the waterfalls, where they were having a picnic. They were very surprised, and pleased, to get a letter there. When they had signed for it, Pat scrambled back to Miss Hubbard. And *then* they had to go all the way back again.

Pat was glad to see his van once more; but what was Jess gazing at, in the back? It was one of George Lancaster's hens – it had got in, somehow, and laid an egg.

"She'll have to stay there until to-morrow," said Pat, "but the egg will do nicely for my tea."

Pat was on his way home when he spotted a sheep stuck in a fence, so he stopped to let it out.

"I think that's my last job for to-day," he said; and off he went.

On his way home he spotted the Thompsons getting their hay in.

"Ooooh, I heard about those sheep in Mr. Jackson's garden," said Alf. "Mr. Jackson was upset! Says he's going to get a new catch on that gate."

"A bit late," said Pat. "If only I'd been twenty minutes earlier, I expect I could have stopped them. Ah well – I'd better be off home now. See you to-morrow. Cheerio!"

"Goodbye, Pat!" they called. "See you to-morrow!"
They were answered by a clucking sound, from the back of Pat's van.

Postman Pat's
Letters on Ice

Greendale was having a hard winter, and there had been still more snow in the night. It was icy as well.

Postman Pat was out on his rounds as usual, but he had to go very carefully.

Sam Waldron was out, too, with his mobile shop.

"Hello, Pat!" called Sam. "Rough weather!"

"Hello, Sam. How is it going?"

"Well . . . I don't think I'll be able to get up to Granny Dryden's with her groceries," said Sam. "I got stuck up there yesterday."

"I'll take them with the letters," said Pat. "My van is good in snow."

"Right-o, Pat, here they are."

Sam handed Pat a box full of groceries: packets of tea, biscuits, butter, bread, flour, bacon, sausages, and a big tin of humbugs.

"That'll keep her going for a while," said Pat.

"Thanks," said Sam. "Mind how you go. Cheerio!"

And Pat was on his way.

The van skidded and slithered along the steep road to Granny Dryden's house.

She was very glad to see him, specially when she saw he had her groceries, as well as a letter. Pat called out cheerfully, as he came in, "Good morning!"

"Oh, thank you, Pat, that's lovely," said Granny Dryden. "I'll not starve, now. And the letter will be from that lass of mine, in London. I cannot find my reading-glasses anywhere – would you tell me what she says, Pat?"

"Certainly. Now . . . let's see . . ."

Pat tore the envelope open, and read aloud. "She says . . . 'Dear Mum, just a line to let you know . . .'"

"Speak up, please, Pat," said Granny Dryden, "I can't hear you."

Pat went on . . . "'We'll all be able to come up to Greendale to see you for your birthday. Jim started school this week, and Dad's bought a new car. All well, and hoping you are, too. All our love, Sally and family.'"

"Ee, that's good news. Thanks, Pat. Have a cup of tea?"

"Thank you, Mrs. Dryden. It's just the thing, this cold weather."

Pat enjoyed his cup of strong hot tea. "Well, I'll be on my way, before it starts snowing again. Goodbye!"

"Bye, Pat!"

Pat's next stop was at Ted Glen's workshop.

"Morning Ted!"
"Hello, Pat."
Ted was busy sawing some wood.
Pat went to warm himself by Ted's stove. "That's a grand stove you've got there," he said. "I could do with that in my van. Ooooooh . . . it's lovely."

He had a letter for Ted. "Here's someone writing from a warm place – Australia!"

"It'll be our Bert," said Ted. "It's ages since he's written. That reminds me . . . I found Bert's old skates this morning. I reckon they'll be just about your size, Pat. Do you fancy trying them? They say the tarn's frozen hard."

Pat looked at the skates doubtfully. "Well . . . I don't know," he said. "I'd love to have a go. Is the ice safe? Has anyone checked it?"

Ted laughed, "Yes, Miss Hubbard, of course. Take them, anyway; you never know when they might come in handy, and I've got some of my own."

"Thanks, Ted. Cheerio!"

Pat was off again, along the snowy roads. The wind was blowing the snow into drifts now, deeper and deeper. Soon, Pat had to stop. The road was blocked with a huge drift of snow. Pat thought he would never get through with his letters now.

Then he looked across to the lake, and saw someone gliding along on the ice. That gave Pat an idea.

"It's worth trying, Jess. I can take a short cut across the lake."

It was George Lancaster, out skating.

"Come on, Pat," he called, "it's lovely."

"You stay here, Jess, and mind the van," said Pat. "I'll just put these skates on."

The skates were a good fit. Pat laced them up firmly, got his bag of letters, and walked carefully out on to the ice.

"Here we go!"

What a time Pat had! He had not skated for years. He toppled and teetered, and nearly fell over, many a time; he went whirling round in circles; he just missed a tree, then had to grab a branch to stop himself.

Somehow, he skated across the lake. Charlie Pringle looked over the wall, and spotted him.

"Hello, Pat," he called. He was very surprised to see Pat arriving on the ice, instead of in his van.

"Hello, Charlie," said Pat. "Special ice-delivery today."

He handed the letters over the wall.

"Thank you," said Charlie. "Good skating!"

Pat whizzed off again. George Lancaster was still on the ice. He did get a surprise when Pat shot by with a letter for him. Mrs. Thompson was out for a spin, too.

When Pat tried to spin round on the ice, he fell down with a bump.

"Hello, Pat," said Mrs. Thompson, "are you all right? What are you doing down there?"

"Yes, I'm all right," said Pat, and gave her some letters.

"Look at Jess," said Mrs. Thompson.

Jess had come to try his paws at skating. Poor Jess, his paws went in all directions at once.

"Come on, Jess," said Pat, "that's enough skating for today. We'll go back on wheels."

Pat backed his van out of the snow drift, and went on his way.

When Pat arrived at the school, there was no one there: they were all snowed-up at home. But they had left a snowman to wait for Pat. Pat had an old envelope in his pocket, so he addressed it to the snowman – Mr. Snowman, The Drift, Greendale School – and tucked it under the snowman's arm. Then the school door opened; it wasn't empty after all!

"Who's that?" said Pat.

It was Ted Glen and Miss Hubbard.

"Hello, Pat," said Miss Hubbard, "have you seen my bike? The snow must have buried it. We'll have to find it – come on!"

They all searched in the deep snow. Pat thought he saw a handlebar sticking out of the snow, but it was only an old kettle. They found the bike at last, and brushed the snow off it.

"Just in time for choir-practice," said Miss Hubbard. "I'll be off now."

Pat opened the gate for her.

"Thank you, Pat. Goodbye!"

"Bye, Miss Hubbard!"

"Nothing stops her, does it?" said Ted.

"See you in church on Sunday," called Miss Hubbard, as she wobbled off along the snowy road.

Pat could hear Jess, miaowing from the van.

"Coming, Jess," he said. "Time to go home." Jess didn't like the cold weather.

"Cheer up, Jess," said Pat. "This snow can't last forever."

Postman Pat's
Breezy Day

It was a breezy day in Greendale. The leaves swirled about the road. The wind blew and buffetted Pat's van as he drove along the valley with the post.

"Hang on, Jess," he said, "it's a right job, driving in this wind."

A scrap of paper blew across his windscreen.

"Help! I can't see!" But Pat managed somehow.

The wind was so strong that people could hardly stand up. They passed Alf Thompson along the road, and he was nearly blown off his feet. He had to hold his hat on with his stick.

Pat drove over the hill, and round a corner, then shouted, "LOOK OUT!" and stood on the brakes.

A tree had blown down, and fallen right across the road. Pat stopped just in time. He got out of the van to have a good look.

"How are we going to get past this lot?"

Jess came to have a look, too. He prowled along the fallen branches. He thought it made a lovely place to climb and play. Pat heard a voice calling from the other side of the tree. "Hello, Pat!" It was Peter Fogg.

"This wretched wind!" he said. "Blowing trees down all over the place. Don't worry, Pat. I'll soon shift it. I'll nip down to the forestry place and borrow their tree-lifting tackle. I won't be long!"

Pat climbed over the wall to have a look at the tree's roots.

"No wonder it blew over," he said. "It's rotten."

Peter was soon back, on his tractor, pulling the log-lifting machine. He had a big power-saw, too.

"Now then, we'll soon cut our way through this. Stand back," he said as he started the power-saw, with a shattering roar, "these things don't half go."

He lopped off the branches, and Pat helped by carrying them into the field. Then Peter sliced the tree's trunk into pieces. The saw cut through the wood at great speed.

"Now then," said Peter, "let's see if we can move it. Phew! It's warm work."

He backed the log-lifter up to the tree. It was like a small crane. He fixed the chain round a piece of the trunk, and started up the motor. It lifted the heavy wood into the air.

Then Peter started the tractor up, and dragged the log into the field. He came back for another piece of tree, and another, until he had cleared a good gap.

"Mmmm, we should be able to get through there," said Pat. He went to get his van . . . but it had gone! Oh! Where could it be? He walked along the road, looking for it. It was quite safe, parked at the side of the road, next to Sam's mobile-shop.

"I moved your van down the road," said Sam. "I could see your new paint was going to get scratched, with all these branches flying about."

"Thanks, Sam," said Pat. "It is smart, isn't it? Royal crown an' all. I'll be on my way now – Peter's managed to clear the road. Cheerio, Sam!"

"Cheerio, Pat!"

Peter was moving the last of the logs. Pat waved to him, and called "Thanks, Peter. Cheerio!" as he went through.

"We'll have to get a move on now, Jess," said Pat. But just as he said it, the engine began to make funny noises.

"Now what?"

The van jerked, coughed, shook, and stopped.

Pat got out and lifted the bonnet to look at the engine. Just as he was bending over to see better, the wind snatched his hat and blew it along the road.

"Help! My hat!"

It rolled along the road, with Pat chasing after it. It blew over the wall, into the stream, and floated away.

"Oh, no!" said Pat. "I'll never catch it now."

He went back to the van. He mended a broken wire, and soon was on his way again.

There was nobody about at the village school.

"Have they all been blown away?" said Pat. Then he saw the children; they were outside enjoying the wind.

But the wind wanted to deliver the letters. It snatched them out of Pat's hand and delivered them in all directions. It blew them across the meadow, behind stones, over walls, and into bushes.

The children helped to find them. One letter was stuck in a tree and Bill Thompson climbed up to get it.

"Careful!" said Pat. "It would be an air-mail letter! What a day! Hold them tightly, I think they're all air-letters today."

Bill took the letters to the headmaster, and Pat waved goodbye.

Pat was blown about the valley all morning, with his letters and parcels. It was almost the end of his windy round, when he saw a flying towel. It was one of Granny Dryden's. He went to help her catch her washing.

It had blown across the garden and planted itself all over the place; in the bushes, amongst the roses, on the lawn, behind the shed . . . everywhere.

"Oh, Pat," said Granny Dryden, "this wind's terrible. You are a dear. I'd never have caught it all by myself. Look, there's more over there."

Pat helped to gather it all in.

"Now we've got my washing," said Granny Dryden, "what about your hat?"

"It blew off miles away," said Pat, "and sailed down a stream."

"Good gracious," said Granny Dryden, "Ted Glen said he'd hooked a postman's hat out of the lake. I didn't see how it could be yours. Look – he popped it on the old scarecrow to dry."

There it was, standing in the next field.

"It looks like mine," said Pat, and walked across for a closer look.
"It is mine!"
He took it off the scarecrow and shook out the creases.
"Thanks, Mr. Scarecrow."

Then he waved to Granny Dryden.

"Time to blow home," said Pat. And off he went. Home to tea with Jess curled up asleep in his basket.